T0072401

# Elizabeth
## Isn't Afraid To Ride Anymore

## Linda Williams Allen

authorHOUSE®

AuthorHouse™
1663 Liberty Drive
Bloomington, IN 47403
www.authorhouse.com
Phone: 1 (800) 839-8640

Published by AuthorHouse    10/14/2015

ISBN: 978-1-5049-0000-3 (sc)
ISBN: 978-1-4969-7499-0 (e)

Print information available on the last page.

# DEDICATION

In loving memory of my mother, Elizabeth Joyce Williams. She believed in me.

This book is dedicated to my grandchildren: Alexia, Asya, Alissia, Caleb, Kailyn, Makenzi and Aiden; my great granddaughter, Brooklynn; and my great nieces: Aiyana, Makenna, Meelah, and Aliviah Faye.

Although this is a true story (written several years ago) about Alexia overcoming her fear of riding the meanest-looking roller coaster ever, it is fun reading for all of you to enjoy! When you are fearful, remember that things may not be as scary as they seem. Granna/Aunt Faye loves you ALL very very much!

Family is everything! Thank you Joseph, my husband; Antonio and Shauna, my son and daughter; and their spouses—with all my love!

A very special honor and appreciation to my best friend,
Gale M. Wilkins. For over 30 years, you have been real.
I love you Gale!

Heartfelt thanks and love goes to all of my family:
especially my dad, Herbert Williams, and my wonderful DC
Metro and North Carolina friends.
I am grateful for all of you.

# Elizabeth
## Isn't Afraid To Ride Anymore

When Elizabeth was a little girl, she regularly visited her grandparents who live near Washington, DC.

They often went to a fun

place called Jeepers.

Jeepers is an indoor,

family entertainment park.

Elizabeth plays lots of games because she can win tickets, which are redeemed for neat gifts and toys.

She always rode the
Tilt-A-Whirl before eating just
in case she got a little dizzy.

The food was delicious. Her favorites were the cotton candy and corn dogs. She was fascinated with the look and feel of the cotton candy. The hardest part was choosing a flavor.

Two of Elizabeth's favorites
are the bumper cars
and the airplane.

She just cannot go to Jeepers

without riding them. In fact,

she loves them so much she

usually rides them many times.

She loves spinning around

and bumping the other kids.

Sometimes she gets to bump

mommies and daddies.

That really makes her

feel like a big girl.

Another one of her favorites

is the soft play area.

The goal is to get to the long, bumpy slides.

This is a huge maze with winding tunnel slides and nets that allow kids to climb in and out.

She screams to the top of
her lungs all the way down and
then goes back for more.

There are five slides, and it's really cool when she and other kids all go down screaming together.

There is one ride that Elizabeth absolutely refused to get on. It is called the Python Pit.

This is a green roller coaster

that looks like a python.

It also goes really fast.

It even goes through a dark cave area. It's not haunted or extremely frightening—just a little too dark for Elizabeth.

Her grandparents always tried

to talk her into riding it, but

she absolutely would not!

One day—much to everyone's surprise—Elizabeth said to her grandfather, "If you will ride with me today, I will ride the Python."

Of course everyone thought that she would chicken out. However, she reluctantly got on; but she held on very tight to her grandfather.

As her grandmother, Granna,
looked on, she could see that
Elizabeth was very afraid
and had begun to cry.

When the ride went into the first pit, she let out a very loud scream; but by the end of the ride she was laughing.

Elizabeth now realizes that

the ride wasn't as fast

as it looked, and she was

very proud of herself.

She even said that she
wanted to ride it again
one day. Needless to say:
"one day" meant "another
day." She was pooped.

Elizabeth was so tired, she decided to save the Skee-ball game for next time.

The last thing was to redeem her tickets. Granna helped her feed the tickets into the ticket-eating machine, and the total count was 431.

Elizabeth chose a pink, heart-shaped jewelry box with a lock; but she needed 1000 tickets for it.

Rather than using her tickets on just anything, she decided to save them until she had enough for the jewelry box and other gifts.

That was a very good decision.

She thanked her grandparents,

and they all headed home.

When they got home, Elizabeth put her coupons—which were proof of the 431 tickets she had won—in a very safe place.

She will add them to what she wins next time and redeem them for large prizes.

Elizabeth was so tired,

she had to take a nap.

## ABOUT THE ILLUSTRATOR

Elysia "Lisa" Netter was born in Ohio in 1995. She has been drawing since early childhood and has always loved art. Elysia is a self-employed artist who specializes in drawing portraits and characters. She currently lives in North Carolina, where she is attending college for Art and Design. Elysia enjoys video games and comic books. She hopes to one day be a video game character artist, where she can bring her art to life.

Printed in the United States
By Bookmasters